CelebriTrees

Historic & Famous Trees of the World

CELEBRITREES

Historic & Famous Trees of the World

Margi Preus

illustrated by
Rebecca Gibbon

Christy Ottaviano Books
Henry Holt and Company ✳ New York

Introduction

Trees are the oldest, biggest, and tallest living organisms on earth. They fire the imagination and inspire wonder and awe. Throughout history, trees were believed to be home to fairies, demons, dragons, dwarfs, spirits, and ancestors.

People love being in, under, and on top of trees. Hollow trees have been used as chapels, post offices, saloons, and homes. Treetops have held orchestras, dining rooms, and party houses.

Trees inspire people to extraordinary achievements. Treaties have been signed, justice dispensed, and the seeds of the American Revolution sown under trees. It is said that Buddha gained enlightenment under the Bodhi Tree.

Here are fourteen Celebritrees, trees so beloved they have earned names for themselves. Many of these trees are still standing. Although we don't know their exact ages, most of them are very, very old. Each tree has a story to tell.

Methuselah

Bristlecone Pine
Inyo National Forest, California
Age: around 4,800 years old

Methuselah is the oldest known single living organism on earth. The tree is so old that when it was first sprouting, the North Pole pointed at the other end of the Little Dipper. Although Methuselah isn't very big or very tall, it has seen more than 59,000 full moons and over 1.75 million sunrises.

Methuselah was already over 200 years old when the ancient Egyptians were building the Great Sphinx.

At a couple of thousand years old, work on the Great Wall of China began. The tree's 4,200th birthday had come and gone before Columbus set foot in the New World.

Methuselah is named for a character in the Bible who was said to have lived for 900 years. If that's the case, the tree has outlived the man by almost 4,000 years.

General Sherman

Giant Sequoia

Sequoia National Park, California

Age: 2,100 to 2,200 years old

The heaviest dinosaur that walked the earth, the Argentinosaurus, weighed 100 tons.

and the tallest was 60 feet tall.

The longest dinosaur was 120 to 170 feet long

But there is a tree that is bigger than all these dinosaurs put together. General Sherman, a giant sequoia, is the biggest living inhabitant of earth by volume. The volume of its trunk alone is over 52,500 cubic feet. At almost three million pounds, it weighs as much as 14 Argentinosauruses, 10 blue whales, or three 747 jets. It is so heavy that if General Sherman could sit on one side of a seesaw, it would take a town of 20,000 people on the other side to raise it. It is so wide that twelve people standing with their arms outstretched can't reach all the way around its trunk. Many of its branches are bigger than any tree growing east of the Mississippi River.

And it is still growing.

Hyperion

Coast Redwood

Redwood National Park, California

Age: unknown

The tallest trees in the world are coast redwoods. From tiny seeds no bigger than tomato seeds, they grow as tall as skyscrapers. Hyperion is the current record holder. At three hundred seventy-nine feet, it is taller than the Statue of Liberty.

Tall trees don't keep their titles for long. Their tops stretch so high that they can be struck by lightning or splintered by wind. They can even get damaged by well wishers. When too many people stood under one of the previous tallest trees, the roots became damaged, and since nutrients could no longer be transported to the uppermost branches, the tree died. Now, exact locations of the tallest trees are not given, to protect them.

Hyperion and the two next tallest trees live in a remote and rugged area of Redwood National Park and probably won't receive many visitors.

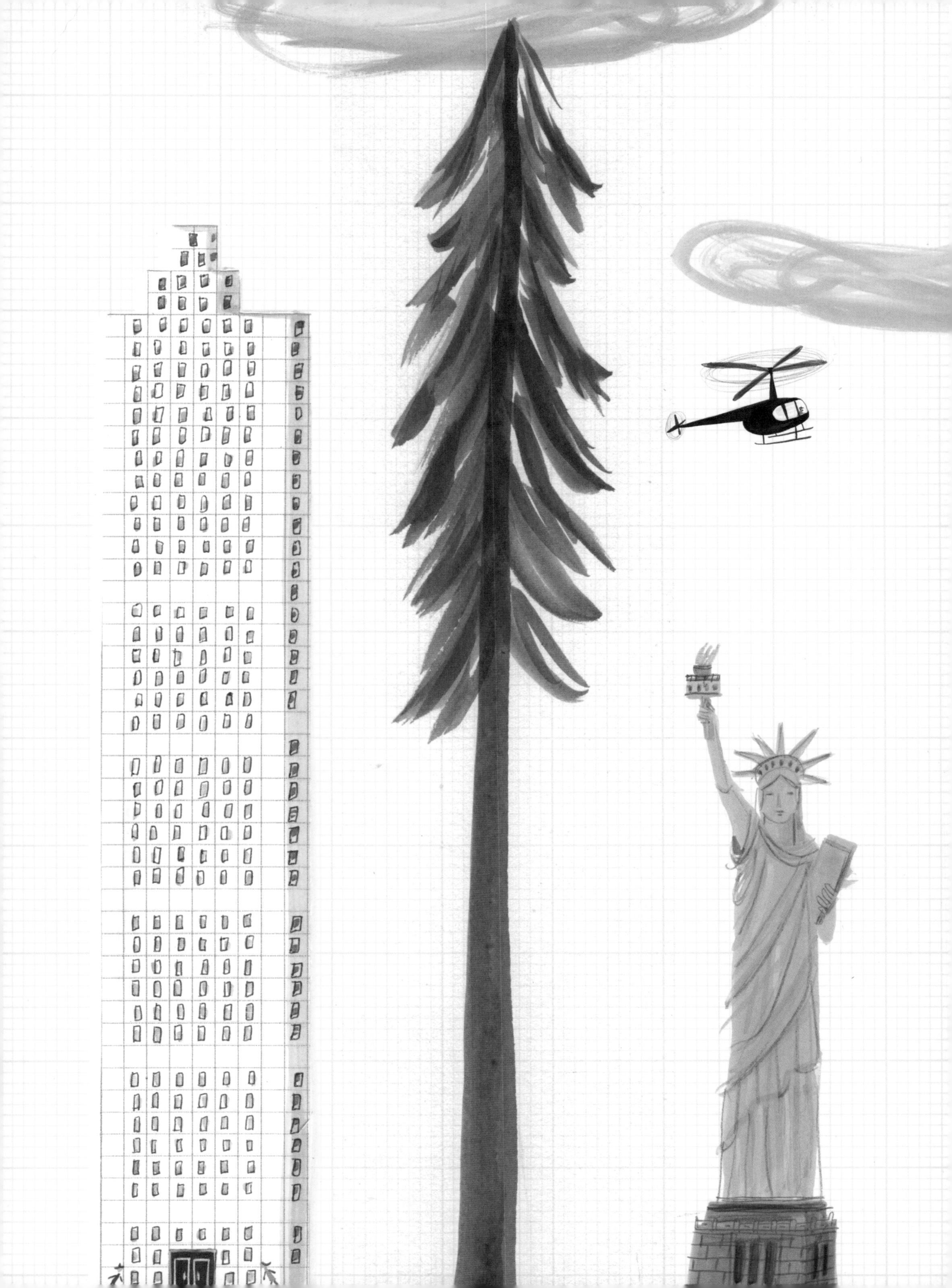

The Tree of One Hundred Horses

Chestnut
Sant'Alfio, Sicily, Italy
Age: 2,000 to 4,000 years old

The Tree of One Hundred
Horses is considered to be the
thickest tree ever known, 190 feet
recorded in 1780. Although now split into
three sections, the 2,000- to 4,000-year-old tree is still alive.

The tree got its name
when, hundreds of years ago,
the Queen of Aragon went sight-
seeing to Mount Etna, a volcano in
Sicily. According to legend, a rainstorm
interrupted the trip, and the queen and all
one hundred horsemen who accompanied her found
shelter under the spreading branches of the huge chestnut tree.

The Tule Tree

Montezuma Cypress
Tule, Mexico
Age: estimated 1,400 years old

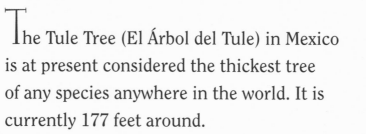

The Tule Tree (El Árbol del Tule) in Mexico
is at present considered the thickest tree
of any species anywhere in the world. It is
currently 177 feet around.

All sorts of knots and contortions of
the bark give the appearance of creatures
hiding inside. Schoolchildren offer a tour
in which they point out the faces of goblins
and monsters, elephants, and even jaguars
in the bark!

The Tule Tree is also a very old tree.
Legend suggests that 1,400 years ago, a
servant to the storm god of the Aztecs
planted it for the people of Tule. Tree
experts agree that the tree is probably
1,400 years old.

The Bodhi Tree

Ficus religiosa
Anuradhapura, Sri Lanka
Age: almost 2,300 years old

The word *bodhi*, a kind of fig tree, can be translated as
"knowledge." The tree is sacred to Buddhists, who believe
that Buddha gained enlightenment while sitting under it.

Today, the most famous "bo" tree grew from a branch taken
from that tree. The king who planted it in 288 B.C.E. prophesied that
it would live forever. Still thriving today, it is probably the most
revered tree in the world.

The Chapel Oak
(Chêne-Chapelle)

Oak
Allouville-Bellefosse, France
Age: said to be 1,200 years old

Hollow trees have found many uses. In 1696 the inside of a huge oak tree in France was made into a chapel. A second chapel was later added upstairs and a large wooden staircase constructed around the outside. A hermit lived in one of the chapels for a time.

Although it has undergone many repairs, the tree is still standing, and it is one of the biggest and oldest trees in France. It continues to serve as a religious monument and a place of pilgrimage. Some 60,000 people visit it every year.

The Major Oak

English Oak
Sherwood Forest, England
Age: estimated 800 to 1,000 years old

It is said that Robin Hood met with his merry men beneath—or maybe inside—the Major Oak, still thriving in Sherwood Forest.

The Major Oak, named after Major Hayman Rooke, is thought to be the largest oak tree in England. The hollow is large enough to hold 12 men, and stories are told of Robin Hood and his men using the tree to hide from pursuers.

Over the years, so many visitors explored the tree that the ground around it became compacted. The roots began to starve. The tree, in danger of dying, was made off-limits and has since recovered. Today, like other old oaks, it performs a service as a miniature nature preserve, providing food and a place to hibernate for bats, queen wasps, butterflies, spiders, and dozens of insect species. Every spring, jackdaws, woodpeckers, great tits, and gray squirrels make their nests in the tree.

Post Office Tree

Bur Oak Council Grove, Kansas

Age: 270 years old

For almost 20 years during the mid-1800s, the hollow in a big bur oak in Kansas was used as an unofficial post office for travelers on the Santa Fe Trail. Settlers moving west left letters and messages in a hole in the base of the tree. People traveling on later wagon trains checked to see if any messages had been left for them.

The tree died in 1990 at 270 years old. Its trunk stood for 18 more years before it was removed.

Dueling Oaks

New Orleans, Louisiana
Age: unknown

Pistols, swords, sabers, bowie knives, shotguns, even poison pills were used as weapons in the many duels that took place in New Orleans in the mid-1800s.

Duels were fought for love, politics, insults, and petty disagreements. A man stepping on a woman's skirt was enough cause for a fight.

Legend has it that a duel was once started because a European scientist insulted the Mississippi River, calling it "a tiny rill compared to the great rivers of Europe." This duel, unlike many others, did not end with a fatality. The European gentleman went home with a slashed cheek as a souvenir.

Most duels in New Orleans took place under the moss-draped branches of a pair of large oaks in City Park. Only one oak remains; the other was lost to the ravages of nature. The surviving oak dueled with Hurricane Katrina in 2005 and came out of the storm bruised, but still fighting.

Scythe Tree

Balm-of-Gilead Poplar
Waterloo, New York
Age: over 150 years

In 1861, the day after attending a recruitment meeting for the Union Army, James Wyman Johnson hung his scythe on the branch of a small poplar tree and said to his parents, "Leave the scythe in the tree until I return." Then Johnson went off to fight in the Civil War.

He never returned, and his heartbroken parents never removed the scythe from the tree. The wooden handle rotted away, but the blade remained.

Some fifty years later, two brothers who lived on the farm enlisted to fight in World War I. The day they left, they hung their scythes in the same tree. When they returned from the war, they removed the handles of the scythes, leaving the blades in the tree.

Even today, tips of all three blades can be seen protruding from the tree. The rest of the blades have been engulfed by the growing wood.

The Boab Prison Tree

Baobab
Derby, Australia
Age: up to 1,000 years old

The baobab tree can grow quite stout. Baobab trees thrive in parts of Africa, Madagascar, and Australia. Often, their fat trunks become hollow. Sometimes this process is helped along by people; they use the hollow trunks to store grain or livestock. In the biggest trees, more than 30,000 gallons of water can be contained in the baobab's spongy wood.

One of the most famous trees in Australia is called the Boab Prison Tree. (Boab is a nickname for the baobab tree.) Stories say that around the turn of the twentieth century up to 10 Aboriginal prisoners would be chained inside the hollow tree.

The Aborigines say the prisoners were chained *outside* the tree. The insides of hollow baobab trees were reserved as sacred resting places for the bones and spirits of their ancestors.

The Tree That Owns Itself

White Oak
Athens, Georgia
Age of new tree: 60 years old

According to legend, young William Jackson spent many happy hours in the branches of an oak tree. He loved the tree so much that when he grew up he deeded the tree to itself, sometime between 1820 and 1832.

"For and in consideration of the great love I bear this tree and the great desire I have for its protection for all time, I convey entire possession of itself and the land within eight feet of it on all sides." With these words the large white oak in Athens, Georgia, became known as the Tree That Owns Itself.

Unfortunately, the original tree fell in a high wind in 1942. But oak trees produce many acorns—about 5,000 per year—and fortunately for the tree, the Athens' Junior Ladies' Garden Club had collected some. One of these acorns was planted and became the current Tree That Owns Itself. It is also known as the Son of the Tree That Owns Itself.

As the famous saying goes, "Tall oaks from little acorns grow" (David Everett, 1769–1813).

ACORNS

Moon Trees

A variety of trees now found
all over the world
Age: less than 50 years old

Trees that have been to the moon?

Stuart Roosa was part of the Apollo 14 trip to the moon in
1971. Before becoming an astronaut he worked for the U.S.
Forest Service and brought hundreds of tree seeds with him on
his voyage in space. The Forest Service and NASA wanted to find
out if being in space and the moon's orbit would have any effect
on the way seeds grew. When he returned to earth, the seeds were
germinated, along with seeds that hadn't been to the moon. Some
of them grew into saplings. No noticeable differences were seen
between moon trees and earth trees.

Since then, "moon trees"
have been planted at the White
House, at Washington Square in
Philadelphia, at Valley Forge, in the
International Forest of Friendship in
Atchison, Kansas, at various universities and
NASA centers, and in countries all over the world.

As long as trees are alive, they keep growing. The trees in this book became Celebritrees because they were allowed to thrive. Given soil, water, sunlight, air, and room to grow, perhaps every tree is a potential Celebritree. You might have one in your own backyard.

MORE ABOUT THE TREES

BRISTLECONE PINES:

Methuselah

Some trees, known as clonal trees, grow from very old roots or plant matter. Old Tjikko, a spruce tree in Sweden, grew from roots that are 9,550 years old. Its stem (or trunk), however, is no more than 600 years old.

Bristlecone pines are trees that grow a single trunk and can become extremely old. They are found high in the White Mountains of California. Many of the oldest live in the Ancient Bristlecone Forest in Inyo National Forest. They grow at high altitudes of 9,000 feet and more. The winter is cold and bitter, the summer is hot and dry, and there is little soil. Even though the trees grow to be scarcely 30 feet tall, they regularly live to be thousands of years old. Amazingly, the oldest trees thrive in the least nutritious soils and reside in the most exposed locations.

Methuselah lives in a grove of trees that are all over 4,000 years old. Only a few people know which tree is the real Methuselah. The tree's identity is kept secret to protect it from vandals.

GIANT SEQUOIA AND REDWOOD:

General Sherman

General Sherman is a giant sequoia, which is a type of redwood tree that grows in California. It is the biggest tree in the world today. The second biggest is General Grant, which commands an area of forest not far from General Sherman. General Grant is the only tree that is a national shrine, dedicated to the men and women who have given their lives in service to this country. It is also the nation's Christmas tree. Services are held under it every Christmas Day.

Some of the sequoias that were cut down in the past were even bigger than the generals. One was so large, 25 men sawed away at it for two weeks before it fell. Its stump was so commodious, it was used as a dance floor for a Fourth of July party in 1854 and was able to accommodate 32 waltzers . . . and the band! In the same era, another slice of a giant sequoia was transformed into a dinner table complete with full place settings of china and crystal for 40 people.

The axe and the chainsaw are the sequoias' worst enemies. Otherwise, these trees are almost indestructible. They are resistant to fungi and insects. Their bark is fire-resistant. In fact, forest fires actually help new seedlings get established.

In spite of their hardiness, however, due to foresting only 3 percent of the ancient redwood forests remain.

COAST REDWOODS:

Hyperion

The coast redwoods of California are the tallest trees in the world. They are also the fastest growing cone-bearing trees in North America and among the oldest living organisms on earth.

Redwoods—or relatives of them— were around in the Jurassic era, when dinosaurs roamed the earth. Though the dinosaurs disappeared, redwoods, in the right environment, continue to prosper.

Compare the redwoods, which grow to be over 300 feet tall, with the smallest trees in the world: arctic birches. Because of the short growing season and the harsh conditions in the Arctic, these trees never grow beyond 10 inches high.

CYPRESS:

The Tule Tree

El Tule is a tree of legend. Stories say that before the Spaniards arrived the tree was able to provide shade for 1,000 people. A bolt of lightning supposedly blasted a hole in it big enough to accommodate twelve men on horseback (the hole later filled in with new wood). It is said that Hernán Cortés cried beneath the Tule Tree and that, hundreds of years later, water flowed like a fountain from one of its branches.

The Tule is a Montezuma cypress, Mexico's national tree. It is also known as Ahuehuete, which means "old man of the water" in the Nahuatl language. Cypress trees like to keep their roots in water and are often found growing near rivers, springs, or swamps.

When people moved to Santa Maria del Tule, they drained the swamp and built streets, houses, and a church. The Tule Tree, deprived of water, was in danger of dying. In the mid-1990s an underground irrigation system was put in place, helping the tree to recover. Lack of water remains an issue for El Tule and other cypress trees nearby, and concerned groups work to maintain its health.

OAK:

Chapel Oak, Major Oak, Dueling Oaks, Post Office Tree, and Tree That Owns Itself

Never stand under an oak tree during a lightning storm. The oak is struck by lightning more than any other kind of tree. Probably because of this tendency, the tree became associated with thunder and thunder gods. It was sacred to Thor, the thunder god of Norse myth, and to the Greek god Zeus, hurler of thunderbolts. Oak groves were places of worship in Germanic rites and for the Druids of the British Isles.

Oak trees have been favorite gathering places for making treaties, having councils, and other important events. In Europe, there are giant oaks still standing whose hollow trunks were so huge they were used as secret courts of justice.

Almost every state in America has at least one famous oak. A grove of white oaks in Jackson, Mississippi, is the founding place of the Republican Party. The Lafitte Oaks of Louisiana's Jefferson Island are said to stand over the buried treasure of the pirate Jean Lafitte. In Connecticut, the now defunct Charter Oak was a hiding place for important government documents. Another famous oak is the Wye Oak of Talbot County, Maryland, which, at 400 years old, 102 feet tall, and nearly 30 feet around, was America's largest oak tree until it was felled by a thunderstorm in 2002.

Each old oak is like a small preserve. According to John Palmer, oak planter and historian, a single large oak can host "over

32 species of mammal, 68 species of bird, 34 species of butterfly, 271 species of insect, 168 species of flower, 10 species of fern, and 31 species of fungi or lichen."

BAOBAB:

The Prison Boab

The baobab has many names. It is often called the Upside-Down Tree because, with its squat trunk and root-like branches, it looks as if its head has been thrust into the earth. It's also known as the Elephant of Plants, Bottle Tree, God's Thumb, and Monkey Bread Tree.

Referred to as the Tree of Life, its fruit and seeds are used as food, its roots and leaves as medicine, and its bark for making ropes, nets, hats, even strings for musical instruments. Hollow baobabs store water, but have also been used as dwellings, bathrooms (complete with plumbing), or even municipal buildings. More than one has been used as a pub, including a boab in South Africa that has hosted up to 60 people.

Moon Trees

Many moon trees were given away with no official record of where they were sent. Now NASA scientist Dave Williams is looking for them. Do you know of any moon trees? Check out the Web site: nssdc.gsfc.nasa.gov/planetary/lunar/moon_tree.html.

MORE ABOUT

Champion Trees

American Forests has maintained the National Register of Big Trees for over 50 years. Using a formula based on circumference, height, and crown spread, American Forests rates trees as champions. If you think you've got a champion, you can learn more about nominating it at this Web site: www.americanforests.org/resources/bigtrees.

What can we do to help grow Celebritrees?

Trees clean the air, shade and cool our homes, help conserve energy, and attract songbirds. Trees filter rainwater into the earth, which helps to prevent floods. They reduce erosion and conserve soil, keeping streams and rivers clean. In some parts of the world, trees hold back encroaching deserts. Trees in coastal forests protect communities from hurricanes and tsunamis.

Trees help us. Here are some ideas on how we can help trees:

- Plant trees. It is important to plant the right tree in the right place and in the right way. Find out what trees are native to your area and how best to plant them before putting them in the ground.

- Take care of the trees you have. All trees need water, especially young trees whose roots are not yet established. Peeling the bark, chopping at trunks, or pulling off branches can hurt or even kill trees.

- Do not take firewood with you when you go camping as it can harbor tree devouring beetles. Use the wood available at the campground.

Paper is made from trees. How can we use less throw-away paper?

- Use a lunch box instead of a paper bag.

- Reuse paper grocery bags at the store or bring your own cloth bags.

- Try to buy products with less packaging.

- Recycle and use recycled products.

If you celebrate Christmas, consider an alternative Christmas tree.

- Try a living tree in a pot that can be planted outside, or a miniature tree that can live inside.

- Designate an outdoor tree as your Christmas tree.

- Sponsor the planting of live trees in a damaged ecosystem (www.americanforests.org/planttrees/holidays.php).

- See more suggestions at www.joytotheplanet.com.

- Join the Tree Musketeers, a national organization of young people who work to improve the environment. You can learn more at www.treemusketeers.org.

Bibliography

Arnold, Caroline. *The Biggest Living Thing*. Minneapolis: Carolrhoda Books, 1983.

Bash, Barbara. *Tree of Life: The World of the African Baobab*. San Francisco: Sierra Club Books, 1989.

Garelick, May, and Barbara Brenner. *The Tremendous Tree Book*. New York: Four Winds Press, 1979.

Hageneder, Fred. *The Meaning of Trees: Botany, History, Healing, Lore*. San Francisco: Chronicle Books, 2005.

Lewington, Anna, and Edward Parker. *Ancient Trees: Trees that Live for a Thousand Years*. London: Collins & Brown, 1999.

Mercatante, Anthony S. *The Magic Garden: The Myth and Folklore of Flowers, Plants, Trees and Herbs*. New York: Harper & Row, 1976.

Meyer, Jeffrey G., with Sharon Linnéa. *America's Famous and Historic Trees: From George Washington's Tulip Poplar to Elvis Presley's Pin Oak*. Boston: Houghton Mifflin, 2001.

Pakenham, Thomas. *Remarkable Trees of the World*. New York: W.W. Norton, 2002.

Rupp, Rebecca. *Red Oaks and Black Birches: The Science and Lore of Trees*. Pownal, Vermont: Storey Communications, 1990.

Vieira, Linda. *The Ever-Living Tree: The Life and Times of a Coast Redwood*. New York: Walker Books, 1994.

Web Sites

American Forests: www.americanforests.org/resources/bigtrees

The Major Oak: www.eyemead.com/majoroak.htm

Moon Trees: nssdc.gsfc.nasa.gov/planetary/lunar/moon_tree.html

In memory of Pépé,
who taught me to love trees
—M. P.

To Jonny:
Thank you for everything!
—R. G.

Henry Holt and Company, LLC
Publishers since 1866
175 Fifth Avenue
New York, New York 10010
www.HenryHoltKids.com

Library of Congress Cataloging-in-Publication Data
Preus, Margi.
Celebritrees : historic and famous trees of the world / by Margi Preus ;
illustrated by Rebecca Gibbon. — 1st ed.
p.   cm.
"Christy Ottaviano Books."
Includes bibliographical references.
ISBN 978-0-8050-7829-9
1. Trees—Juvenile literature. 2. Champion trees—Juvenile literature.
3. Historic trees—Juvenile literature. I. Gibbon, Rebecca. II. Title.
SD383.P74 2010   582.16—dc22   2009029318

First Edition—2010 / Designed by April Ward
The artist used acrylic ink, colored pencil, and watercolor on
acid-free cartridge paper to create the illustrations for this book.
Printed in November 2010 in China by Toppan Leefung Printing Ltd.,
Dongguan City, Guangdong Province, on acid-free paper. ∞

1 3 5 7 9 10 8 6 4 2